King
Arthur's
Courage

by Stephanie Spinner
illustrated by Valerie Sokolova

A STEPPING STONE BOOK™
Random House New York

For Rena
—S.S.

To my sister Lanna when she was a little girl
—V.S.

Text copyright © 2002 by Stephanie Spinner. Illustrations copyright © 2002 by Valerie Sokolova. All rights reserved under International and Pan-American Copyright Conventions. Published in the United States by Random House Children's Books, a division of Random House, Inc., New York, and simultaneously in Canada by Random House of Canada Limited, Toronto. Originally published by Golden Books, an imprint of Random House Children's Books, a division of Random House, Inc., New York, in 2002.

www.steppingstonesbooks.com
www.randomhouse.com/kids

Library of Congress Cataloging-in-Publication Data
Spinner, Stephanie.
King Arthur's courage / by Stephanie Spinner ; illustrated by Valerie Sokolova.
    p.   cm. — (A Stepping stone book fantasy)
SUMMARY: King Arthur tells the Knights of the Round Table a tale of his capture and betrayal by his half-sister, Morgan le Fay.
ISBN 0-307-26410-6 (trade) — ISBN 0-307-46410-5 (lib. bdg.)
1. Arthur, King—Juvenile literature. 2. Arthurian romances—Adaptations. [1. Arthur, King—Legends. 2. Knights and knighthood—Folklore. 3. Folklore—England.]
I. Sokolova, Valerie, ill. II. Title. III. Series.
PZ8.1.S7672Ki   2005   398.2'0942'02—dc22   2004007636

Printed in the United States of America   11 10 9 8 7 6 5 4 3 2

RANDOM HOUSE and colophon are registered trademarks and A STEPPING STONE BOOK and colophon are trademarks of Random House, Inc.

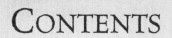

Contents

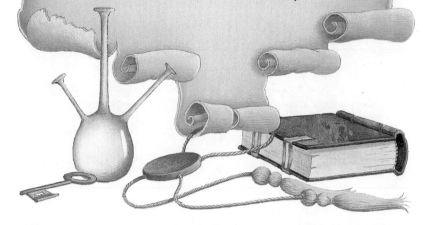

Arthur at the Round Table

I am Arthur Pendragon, King of England. At the heart of my court is the Round Table. It is a place where heroes meet—dragon slayers, glory seekers, knights scarred in battle. Each one has a tale to tell.

Always, when I listen, I forget I am king. Such is the power of a good story.

From time to time, silence falls over the Table. Then I think to tell a story of my own.

But I never have—until now.

One morning in spring, I went out hunting. Sir Accolon rode with me.

Just before sunrise, a great stag appeared out of the trees. We gave chase. It outran us. Whenever we drew close, it slipped into the shadows. Then we would see it again, a little farther away.

Our horses were swift and strong,
but the stag stayed always out of reach.
On and on we rode. Before long, we
were far from Camelot.

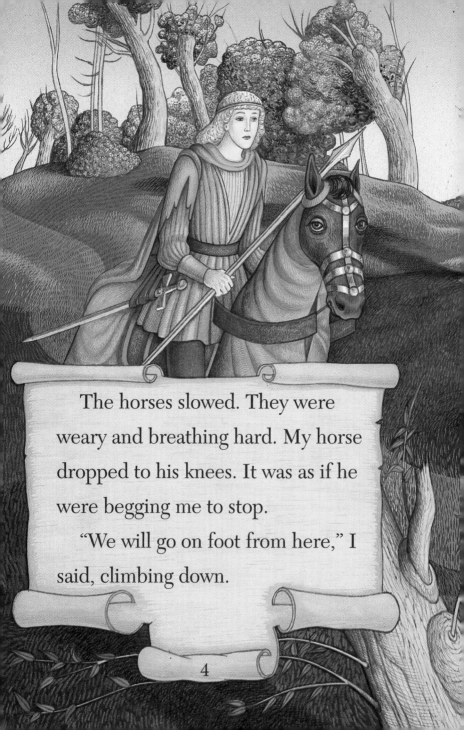

The horses slowed. They were
weary and breathing hard. My horse
dropped to his knees. It was as if he
were begging me to stop.

"We will go on foot from here," I
said, climbing down.

4

"Where, my lord?" asked Accolon.

"Where, indeed," I replied. I looked around. I hoped for some familiar sign, but found none.

We were lost.

Chapter Two

At that moment, a ray of sunlight came gliding through the trees. It lit a path for us and we took it. Soon we reached a lake as bright as polished steel.

I spotted a ship in the distance. It moved swiftly across the water and stopped on shore before us.

"By the saints!" Accolon whispered in surprise.

I, too, was surprised. The ship was empty. *Is no one steering this ship?* I wondered.

Aloud I said, "Let us go aboard."

We stepped onto the deck. And then, though it was noon, night fell. We waited in fear, but only for an instant. Suddenly, a hundred torches blazed. In their welcome light, twelve damsels appeared.

"Greetings, King Arthur!" they said. "Your visit honors us!"

"You know me?" I asked. None of

them answered. Instead, they led us to a room on the ship. There a table was set for two.

"Sit," said one of the damsels.

"Rest," said another, and they drew our chairs for us.

"Drink," said a third, pouring wine from a flask of gold.

"Eat," said yet another. Before us was enough food for ten men.

"What magic is this?" whispered Accolon.

"It is like a dream," I said. Yet my hunger and thirst were real.

Accolon began to eat. "The food is good," he said.

And so it was. We ate and drank our fill, speaking little. Soon I was so weary that I could not speak at all.

I longed for sleep. At that moment, the torches dimmed. Then the damsels led us to a chamber where two beds waited.

In darkness, we sank down—into the sleep of the bewitched.

Chapter Three

I dreamed that my sister, Morgan le
Fay, stood before me. Her hair flew
around her face like dark lightning.
Her eyes were wide with anger.

Morgan and I had the same mother.
Yet we were never at ease with each
other, as a brother and sister should be.

"Why do you hate me?" I asked sadly.

Her mouth twisted into a smile. "I do not hate you, brother," she said. "How can you think that?"

I knew she was lying.

Then I woke and hoped I was still dreaming.

Gone were the damsels with their smiles. Gone were the golden flasks and the silken sheets.

Gone, too, was my sword, Excalibur.

I was no longer on the ship. I was in a stone cell on a bed of filthy straw. There were chains on my ankles and twenty men around me. They were a sorry group, as thin as lances. Accolon was not among them.

"Who are you?" I asked them.

"Prisoners of Lord Damas," said a man with dark hair. "He is lord of this castle, and a knight without honor."

"Why are you his prisoners?"

"He wanted us to fight his brother, and we would not," the dark-haired man said.

"His brother is a good knight named Ontzlake," said a man with blue eyes. "Damas has taken Ontzlake's land. He has taken Ontzlake's castle. He longs to take Ontzlake's life, but fears to meet him in combat."

"Damas is a coward," the dark-haired man said. "He asked each of us to fight Ontzlake for him. When we refused, he locked us up."

"He gives us no food," said a man from the corner. His voice was weak.

"Seven have died here," said the man with the blue eyes.

That is seven too many! I thought. Then I heard my name. "Arthur," a young woman called from the door of our cell, "how do you fare?"

"I would fare better without these chains," I replied.

"They will be taken off," she said, "if you will fight for Lord Damas."

"I will not," I said.

"Alas," she said, turning away. The man in the corner let out a ragged cough. Another moaned softly.

I could not bear their suffering.

"Wait!" I called to her. "I will fight—
if Lord Damas frees these men." I
pointed to the knights in the cell.

"I will tell him," said the woman.
She hurried away.

Then word came that Damas would
free the men. As for me, I would fight
Lord Ontzlake.

Chapter Four

The next day, we were led out of prison. Some of the knights stumbled blindly in the sun. Others knelt to touch the grass. The man with dark hair bowed to me.

"We owe you our lives," he said.

I was brought armor, a lance, and a horse. As I climbed onto the saddle, a serving woman came up to me.

"Your sister sends her love," she said, "and this with it." Then she gave me Excalibur, my sword. *Now I cannot lose*, I thought. Excalibur was magical. It had saved my life more than once. Today it would save me again.

"Send thanks to my sister," I said. *Could it be that she did not hate me?* My heart leaped at the thought.

When I rode onto the field, Lord Damas motioned for silence.

"Hail my champion," he called out, "who fights for me this day!" He raised

his arm to lead a cheer. The crowd kept silent.

They hate him, I thought.

The horns blew. At the signal, I spurred my horse and raised my lance. Ontzlake rode at me. I was ready to strike.

He hit me first.

I fell back, breathless. His blow was like a heavy rock crushing my chest.

But I had hit him, too. I felt my lance strike. I heard the clash of wood against metal. His groan told me that I did not fall alone.

Ontzlake was on his feet quickly. I drew my sword. Before he could strike, I struck him.

Excalibur's magic, I thought, *will end this soon.*

I was wrong.

He stood calmly, as if he felt nothing. I had attacked with all my strength, yet Ontzlake was unharmed.

Then he struck back. His sword
sliced through my shield like an ax
through wood. Even as it cut me
deeply, I wondered at its sharpness.

In great pain, I struck again. Again my sword was useless against him. Then he struck, and his sword broke mine.

But how? Excalibur could not be broken!

I staggered, feeling a chill of fear. My sister—false Morgan le Fay—had not given me Excalibur. She had lied, just as she had lied in my dream. Morgan had given me a flimsy, brittle sword—a plaything.

And my sword, Excalibur?

It was in the hands of my foe.

Chapter Five

Without a sword, my only weapon was my shield. Before I could raise it, Ontzlake attacked again.

"Let him rest!" called the crowd.

One man cried, "Make peace, you brothers!"

Yet Lord Damas said nothing, and Ontzlake kept coming.

He struck again, and I fell. For less than a breath, I saw a lake and a fair lady upon it. She was the Lady of the Lake, who had given me Excalibur. But when I opened my eyes she was gone, and I was on the ground.

"Surrender!" said my foe. He held Excalibur to my throat.

"I will not," I said.

"Then prepare to die," he said.

"Have mercy!" voices called from the crowd. "You cannot kill him! He is unarmed!"

But I was not unarmed. I still had my shield. With the last of my strength, I thrust it at Ontzlake. Surprised, he fell back. Excalibur dropped from his grasp.

My sword! I thought, rising. And like a living thing, it flew into my hand. *You have been gone from me too long.* I gripped Excalibur, and it steadied me.

This made my heart glad.

Newly strong, I struck Ontzlake with the force of lightning hitting a hollow tree. He sank with a cry of pain. Then he tried to rise, but could not.

I did not want to kill him. The knights had told me Ontzlake was a good man. I took off his helmet.

Then I truly did not know what to do. For the knight at my feet was not Ontzlake.

He was my own man, Accolon.

Chapter Six

"Accolon!" I cried. "Who gave you my sword?" I raised Excalibur.

"Your sister," he said. "Morgan le Fay."

For a moment I could not speak.

"She told me she loved me," said Accolon. "She promised that if I killed you, she would marry me. Then, as

queen, she would make me her king."
Accolon's voice fell to a whisper. "I
loved her. I agreed."

"And Ontzlake?" I asked. "Where is
he?"

"Morgan used her magic to keep
him from the field." He pointed to a
tent at the edge of the woods. "She

sent me instead." Tears filled his eyes. "Fair lord, I beg your mercy."

I looked at Accolon with pity. Did Morgan truly love him? I did not think so. He had believed her lies, just as I had. Now his life was fading away.

"I grant you mercy," I said. "You meant me harm, but I believe my sister used her dark powers to turn you against me." I put down my sword.

Accolon's breath came hard. "Thank you, my lord," he whispered.

With my help, he raised his head. "All you gathered here," he called, "this brave knight is King Arthur, my ruler and yours. For fighting him and wounding him, I am truly sorry."

Accolon's words caused a great stirring in the crowd. I called for Damas to come before me.

"Damas," I said, "your people like you not at all. You have caused many to suffer. First among these is your brother, Ontzlake. From this day forth, he will own this castle and these lands. He will rule your people for you."

"My lord—!" gasped Damas. He could not believe my words.

"You will carry no weapons," I told him, "not even a dagger. Those men

who served you will serve you no
longer."

Damas shook his head.

"If I learn that you have not obeyed,"
I said, "you shall die."

"Yes, Your Majesty," said Damas.

I sent one of the knights to lead Ontzlake from the tent. He came forward and bowed.

"Rise, Lord Ontzlake," I said, "and do as I bid you. First bring peace to this land, which has seen only strife for many years. Then join me at the Round Table. I will keep a place for you there."

"I will do so with great joy," said Ontzlake, and the crowd cheered.

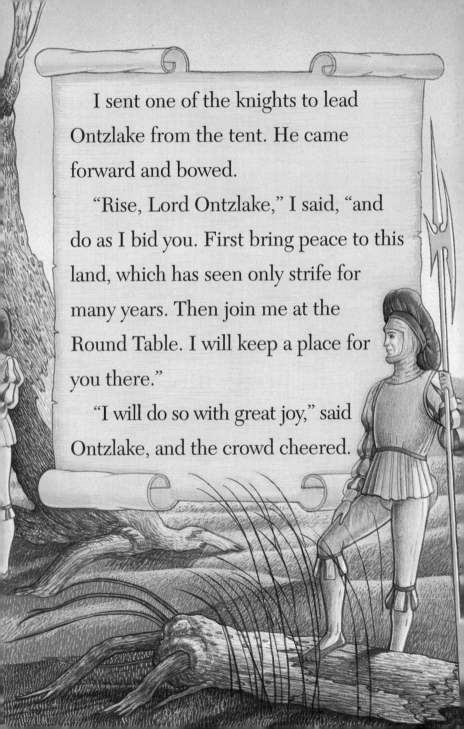

Chapter Seven

Accolon and I were taken to an abbey near the castle. There our wounds were tended. Mine began to heal. Accolon's did not. Before he died, he asked to be buried in the forest where we had hunted.

"You have my word on it," I said.

I sent his body back to Morgan with

six loyal knights. "Tell my sister of Accolon's last wish," I said. "Tell her also that my sword, Excalibur, is once again in its rightful place."

When I was strong enough, I rode back to Camelot. I took my seat at the Round Table and said nothing of my adventure.

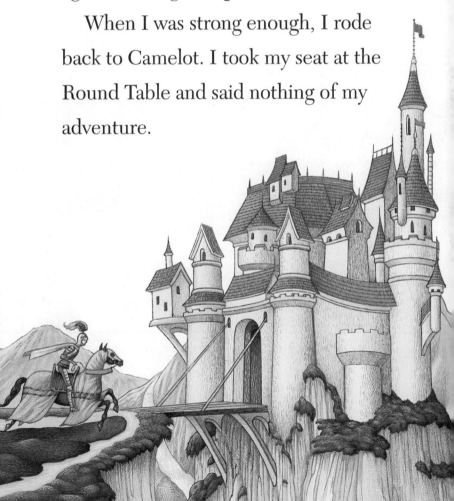

At sunset, I found Accolon's grave. There knelt Morgan, weeping. Her eyes were shut. Her face was wet with tears. Surprised, I kept my distance.

I do not think she saw me. If she did, she gave no sign.

No word of these events has ever passed between us. Nor did my sister Morgan ever again speak poor Accolon's name.

And from that day on, my sword, Excalibur, has never left my side.

Arthur at the End
of His Days

I sought many things in my life. I looked for adventure and found it. I found love. I even found the wisdom to be a good king. For a few happy years, there was peace in England. Of that I am proud.

But the one thing I never found was peace with my sister Morgan.

I regret that still.

AUTHOR'S NOTE

Did King Arthur really exist? A book from 1136 called *A History of the Kings of Britain* says he did. It lists Arthur as a warrior king of the fifth century.

Whether or not he really lived, there are many wonderful songs, plays, and poems about Arthur. In some he is a good-hearted boy who became a great king. In others, he is a man who loved adventure more than he loved ruling.

In all of them, he is an example of what a king should be—kind, brave, and devoted to his people.